Bubble, Bubble

Written and Illustrated by
Amber McClung

tate publishing
CHILDREN'S DIVISION

Published by Tate Publishing & Enterprises, LLC
127 E. Trade Center Terrace | Mustang, Oklahoma 73064 USA
1.888.361.9473 | www.tatepublishing.com

Tate Publishing is committed to excellence in the publishing industry. The company reflects the philosophy established by the founders, based on Psalm 68:11,
"The Lord gave the word and great was the company of those who published it."

Published in the United States of America

ISBN: 978-1-68254-515-7
1. Fiction / General
2. Humor / General
16.03.01

This book belongs to:

_____

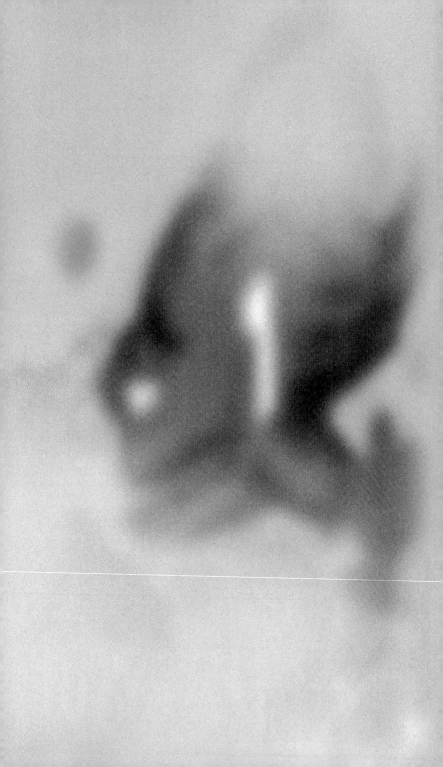

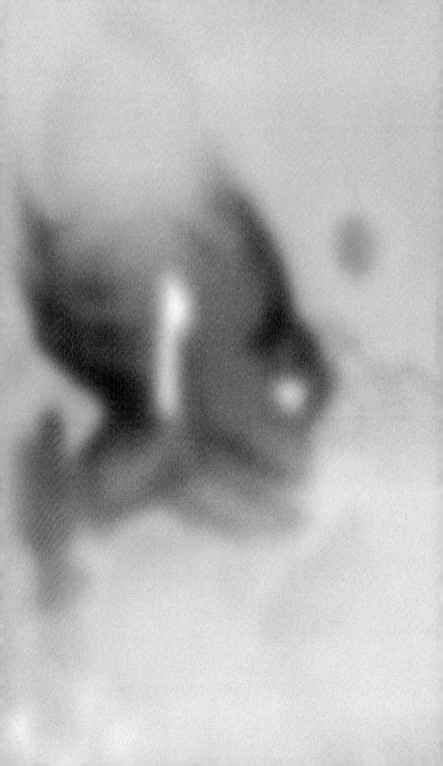

CPSIA information can be obtained
at www.ICGtesting.com
Printed in the USA
LVOW01s0909300816
502372LV00010B/30/P